GENIUS JOLENE

GENIUS JOLENE

Sara Cassidy

ILLUSTRATED BY
Charlene Chua

orca Echoes

ORCA BOOK PUBLISHERS

Library and Archives Canada Cataloguing in Publication
Title: Genius Jolene / Sara Cassidy; illustrated by Charlene Chua.
Names: Cassidy, Sara, author. | Chua, Charlene, illustrator.
Series: Orca echoes.
Description: Series statement: Orca echoes
Identifiers: Canadiana (print) 20190169141 | Canadiana (ebook) 2019016915X |
ISBN 9781459825291 (softcover) | ISBN 9781459825307 (PDF) |
ISBN 9781459825314 (EPUB)
Classification: LCC PS8555.A7812 G46 2020 | DDC jC813/.54—dc23

Library of Congress Control Number: 2019947367
Simultaneously published in Canada and the United States in 2020

Summary: In this illustrated early chapter book, Jolene travels to Los Angeles with her father, a long-haul trucker.

Orca Book Publishers is committed to reducing the consumption of nonrenewable resources in the making of our books. We make every effort to use materials that support a sustainable future.

Orca Book Publishers gratefully acknowledges the support for its publishing programs provided by the following agencies: the Government of Canada, the Canada Council for the Arts and the Province of British Columbia through the BC Arts Council and the Book Publishing Tax Credit.

Cover artwork and interior illustrations by Charlene Chua
Author photo by Katrina Rain

ORCA BOOK PUBLISHERS
orcabook.com

Printed and bound in Canada.

23 22 21 20 • 4 3 2 1

For Dale, Pam, Rowan and Siobhan, who understand the joys of adventure, family and love.

Chapter One

Dad, Joey and I step out of the apartment building into the cool night. A streetlamp hums above us, and the enormous Freightliner rumbles at the curb. It isn't actually allowed on most city streets because it weighs so much. As much as a school bus carrying eight elephants, Dad likes to say.

Joey hands me my backpack. "You pack too light," he says.

"I pack what I need," I tell him. "Four underwear, four T-shirts, a hoodie and the jeans I'm wearing."

"No swimsuit?"

"Underwear."

"Pajamas?"

"One of Dad's T-shirts."

Joey shakes his head. "You'll get cold."

"It's nearly summer!" I cry.

But Joey's already running back into the apartment building. I look at Dad and smirk. He shrugs. Then he yanks open the door of the truck's cab, and I scramble up.

My side of the eighteen-wheeler is completely different from his. It's duller than a waiting room. The biggest excitement is the glove compartment.

But Dad's side is a party. A cockpit with dials and levers and switches

and gauges and two radios and a navigation screen. His huge chair goes up and down and back and forth, and it has a switch that makes the seat as hard as cement or as soft and fluffy as a cloud.

It's a strict rule that I stay on my side. I'm allowed to reach over to turn on the fan if the cab is sweltering, or to change the radio station if the news is too sad, but that's it.

While Dad waits for Joey, I arrange my blanket around me and strap myself in. Cozy. Dad's beaded keychain, which I made for him at out-of-school care, sways from the ignition switch.

A blue cardboard tree dangles from the fan. It's called an air freshener, but, as Joey says, it doesn't make the air fresh; it just smells it up with something different.

What kind of stink would blue be? Blueberry? I rub the tree, then put my fingertips to my nose. The smell makes my throat itch like the school janitor's floor cleaners do.

Joey comes out of the apartment building with a plastic shopping bag stuffed full of clothing. I spy the sash from my fuzzy bathrobe and my least favorite pair of pajamas, the ones with the too-tight waistband.

On the sidewalk Joey and Dad talk like strangers.

"Have a safe trip," Joey says to Dad.

"We'll be on the number 19 all the way," Dad tells him. "That highway's designed for safety. It's lit up at night like a video game. We can't go wrong."

"Call when you can," Joey says. Then softly he adds, "Okay?"

"I will," Dad says. He steps toward Joey. They clap each other on the back. Then, quick as a sniff, as a bird darting from one tree to another, they kiss on the lips right there on the street.

Dad opens his door and hops into his seat, whistling. He winks at me and puts the truck in gear.

"He's going to be mad," I say as we pull away.

"About what?" Dad looks in the side mirror and sees the bag on the ground. "Whoops. Well, I'm not turning this rig around now."

We drive past the rec center and my school. A school at night, with no kids or teachers, is the emptiest thing. The store on the corner with the fifty-cent candy bags is dark, except for the pop machine deep inside, lit up like a heart. I snap a photo.

"I'm hungry," I say.

"I'm *starving*," Dad growls.

We burst out laughing. Because didn't Joey just feed us a pile of scrambled eggs and a stack of toast and a "Hollywood hill" of beans?

When Dad and I are on the road, we eat. We do it well. We go to places we've never been before and order meals we've never tried. We eat like it's homework. We compare the bacon avocado burger to the picture in the ad. We break open the battered codfish and poke at it with a fork to see just how flaky it is. We try the latest salad dressing instead of always asking for Thousand Island.

Every year we choose something to try at each place we go. One year it was hash browns. Another year it was milkshakes. We take notes and rate the items on a scale of one to ten, and at the end of the trip we declare a winner.

Last year we tested cheeseburgers. We ate them at all the big restaurant chains, but the best burger appeared at a community baseball game. The patty was thick and juicy, and the bun was just the right size. Not so thick that it overtakes the meat, and not so thin that it goes mushy with ketchup and meat juice. The best part was the cheese.

"Remember the blue cheese?" I ask as Dad pulls the truck onto the highway.

"I will never forget it," Dad answers. "We thought we were headed to a baseball game, but it turned out to be cheeseburger heaven."

"My idea is we do onion rings this year."

"Genius," Dad says, smiling his one-gold-tooth smile. "Genius Jolene."

Purple seeps into the dark sky. It's dawn. Then it will be morning. Then afternoon. Then evening. Then night again. Driving is simple like that. All you have to do is watch, and everything changes around you.

We're coming up to my favorite sign. I take a picture as we rumble past. *You are leaving Martinville*, the sign says.

On the other side of the highway is a sign for people going the opposite direction. It reads *Welcome to Martinville*. But there's a gap between the two signs, a long few seconds where you've both left Martinville and still are in Martinville. Over the years I've tied my brain in knots trying to make sense of that impossible place.

Chapter Two

I've done long-haul trips with Dad since I was four years old. I wasn't even in kindergarten then and rode along in a booster seat. Now, though, I don't need a booster seat, and I have to miss school. I love school, but I super love going on the road with Dad.

He tells the teacher he needs me with him. That's what he says. Not that he *wants* me on the road, but that he *needs* me. "Can you put together some schoolwork for her to do on the road?" he asks.

Usually the teacher gives me a book to read and a brown envelope thick with worksheets. But last week, in addition to that, Ms. Formosa opened a drawer in her desk and pulled out an old-style digital camera. "This is homework too. Well, truck work," she said. "I want you to take three photos a day of things that strike you as important. I don't care what makes them important. Beautiful is important. But so is ugly. If it makes you feel happy or sad, or makes you think or wonder, take a picture. If it matters to you, it's important."

I immediately turned on the camera and took a picture of Ms. Formosa. She laughed. Then she raised an imaginary

camera and snapped a photo of me. It was like we'd hugged each other.

"When you get back," she said, "we'll put your photos on the big screen, and you can tell us all about your trip."

It's cool riding in the truck, so high up that the rabbits in the ditches are as small as mice. Friends ask if it's boring, but it's not. There's always something to see or think about. I get a kind of royal feeling up here, like I can look out over the world and make decisions about it.

"Looks like it's going to rain," Dad says as we pass a farmer's field. "The cows are lying down."

I watch as a cow lowers herself onto her front knees and then her back knees. Dark clouds are collecting in the sky above. I look at the cow again, her belly on the grass, and I figure something out.

"I know why they lie down," I say. "To keep a spot dry for when it starts to rain. Who wants to lie in wet muck?"

Dad clucks. "Genius Jolene strikes again!"

We never see the rain. We drive out from under the storm clouds, and soon they're behind us in the big side mirror.

Dad lets me open Google Maps on his phone and figure out where we're going. We don't have to do anything for a whole week except barrel south to Los Angeles, then turn around and head home again. The truck is loaded with gigantic rolls of newsprint that we're delivering to a big newspaper company. The paper will get inked and cut and folded into newspapers. After we drop off the rolls, we'll load up with something else to bring back home.

I stare at the stinky tree dangling on its string. Whenever Dad turns a corner, it swings in circles. The tree's stink makes my nose tickle and my throat itch, but I don't mention it.

Because everything else is absolutely perfect.

Chapter Three

"I'm going to start gnawing on my own arm if we don't eat now," Dad says, pulling the rig off the highway and into a truck stop. A truck stop is where truckers can take a shower, do laundry, fill up with gas and park for the night. There's nearly always a restaurant where you can grab a meal.

Climbing down from the cab and touching pavement is a bit like getting

off the ice after skating. My body feels
like it's still moving. I wait a moment to
get settled. Birds chirp in the trees on the
edge of the parking lot, and the tall grass
whistles in the morning breeze. I feel far
from home already.

The restaurant is called Wheelers.

"They're the frozen kind," the server tells us when we order the onion rings. "They are not like my mama made."

"And how was that?" Dad asks.

"The same. But entirely different."

"That was enlightening," Dad jokes once the server has moved on. From his shirt pocket he pulls out the little notebook he calls his log. He writes down how far we've traveled and how long we've been on the road.

"Doesn't the new computer keep track of that?" I ask. "With the GPS?"

"The Grand Poobah System. Yes, it does." Dad licks the tip of his pencil. "But habit is habit."

"Here you go, hon."

I lift my elbows, and the server puts down a box of crayons and a paper place mat with games on it. There's a word

21

search and a crossword and a "find ten differences."

There's also a little frame where you're supposed to draw a picture of yourself. I start with my hair, brown with some curl, halfway down my back. I draw my freckles and my straight-across eyebrows. Joey likes the shape of my eyebrows. "It's easy to tell when you're mad," he says, "because they just slope down. It's also easy to tell when you're happy."

I draw my mouth, which is kind of full and round. My eyes are green, so that's easy. And my eyelashes are thick and stubby, like the bristles on a vacuum cleaner. My nose ends up looking like a melting pyramid though. Noses are ridiculous.

"Your hair's not that long," Dad says.

I scowl at him.

"Not yet?" he squeaks.

A few months ago I got my hair tangled in Mom's brush. Mom had to *cut* the brush out, which left my hair pretty short.

"It's a bob," she said, standing back, scissors in hand. "Very stylish."

"I don't care about stylish," I said.

Mom left the bathroom. I sat there with the towel over my shoulders and

my hair combed wet against my scalp and waited. I thought she was getting hair oil or a hand mirror so I could see my hair from the back. But Mom never came back. That's how she's been since she and Dad divorced a year ago. She is always getting distracted and wandering off.

I live with Mom for one week, then with Dad and Joey for a week. I have a bedroom at each apartment, and it's okay. The apartments are close enough to each other that I can walk between them whenever I want to, and I didn't have to change schools like some kids do when their parents separate.

There's a kid at school who lives two weeks with each parent, and I think that would be better. But Dad thinks I'd start to miss him, and Mom thinks I'd start to miss her. I told them I wouldn't, and so they confessed that it's *them* who would miss *me*. We're going to try it when I'm ten though.

When everything was happening, Mom and Dad got me a book about divorce. But in the book, the parents fight and the kids put their hands over their ears and cry. That never happened with us. Fighting isn't why Mom and Dad divorced.

They sat me down one Sunday morning at the kitchen table. "Daddy doesn't love me the way married people love each other," Mom said.

"So not in a romantic way," I said. "Just friends."

"Right," Mom said. "But there's something else."

"What?"

"I think it's men I'm supposed to love that way," Dad said.

I was so surprised I couldn't talk. I knew what gay people were and what it meant. But Dad? I had just never thought of it.

I looked at Mom. "Are you mad about it?" I asked.

She shook her head. "I'm not mad. In fact, I'm even proud of your dad. And I'll be happy for him too, once I get past being sad for me." Tears leaked out of her eyes, and narrow rivers ran down her cheeks. Her nose turned red.

Dad got off his chair, kneeled down and put his arms around her waist. "I'm so sorry," he said.

"I know." Mom's voice was thick with tears.

My heart throbbed like a bruise. "How do you know you love men?" I asked him.

"I think I always have," he answered. "But I was scared. I'd be the first gay person in my family—the first one who told anyone they were, anyway. Some people have strange ideas about gay people. They think we're unnatural."

"You're natural," I said.

"Well, thank you," Dad said.

"There's something else," Mom said. "Daddy's met someone who he loves in the romantic way."

"I don't want to meet him," I said, crossing my arms the way I do when I don't want to eat something.

That made my parents laugh. Then I laughed too. We were laughing and crying at the same time. It really can happen.

I met Joey two months later. He's really calm and organized. He plays hockey and cooks vegetarian food, and he's Coast Salish, which means he is Indigenous. His family has lived in our area for *thousands* of years.

Dad's apartment was a total mess before Joey moved in. His balled-up socks were all over the place, and there was never a clean glass for water. The toothpaste tube would be squeezed right out for weeks. I once had to cut the tube with nail scissors just to get a drop of green gunk on my toothbrush.

Joey made me a reading nook. It's a couch under a window, with extra cushions and a warm blanket and a lamp and shelves for books. He got a little wooden box that always sits on the top shelf. It's to hold my library card, so now I always know where it is. The coolest thing, though, is the tray with a kettle, two mugs and a basket of hot-chocolate packets. I can make myself a hot chocolate anytime I want.

Joey loves to read. Sometimes he joins me in my nook and reads his book, or we'll go through my latest batch from the library, taking turns reading chapters out loud.

Mom lives in our old apartment. She was sad for a long time. She watched Netflix every evening. Sometimes I'd wake up in the middle of the night and she'd still be watching. But then one day she put on Beyoncé and started making

coconut chocolate-chip cookies, my favorite. She let me lick the spoon, and while the cookies baked we danced in the kitchen. Mom picked me up, and I wrapped my legs around her waist like I hadn't done since I was six.

"You're happy!" I said.

"Yep, I am. It's like someone washed the windows and I can see again. Everything is going to be fine, Jolene. For all of us."

When she said that, my heart rose to the surface. I didn't even know it had been lurking at the bottom, like those fish so deep in the ocean they eventually go blind.

"Here you are." The server puts our meals in front of us. As well as onion rings, Dad's having a BLT and I'm having a grilled cheese.

"One year we'll have to rate coleslaw," Dad says, poking at the foamy green mound on his plate. "This stuff would get zero."

The onion rings are in a plastic basket. Dad and I each take one and tap them like grown-ups clink their glasses of wine. "Onto the palate and into the belly," we say. The palate is the tasting part of the tongue.

I turn my place mat over and make notes in crayon.

Wheelers onion rings:
Dark brown. Hard. Thick batter.
Flavor: "No taste of onion" —Dad
"Not greasy enough" —Jolene
Notes: Server said they were frozen and that her mother's homemade ones were better. We like that they're crispy-crunchy, but that's all.

Dad: 5/10
Jolene: 6.5/10

"I'd give them a three myself," says the server, taking our plates. "Sorry to read over your shoulders."

Chapter Four

Once we're back in the truck, Dad turns on the radio, and I do homework. There's a bit of reading, a quiz about how seeds grow, ten math sheets that I gobble up since I'm crazy about math, and a poem by Robert Frost to memorize called "Stopping by Woods on a Snowy Evening."

The poem is about a person in the old days stopping their horse carriage just to watch snow fall on a forest. The person's horse is confused. Why would his owner stop in the middle of nowhere on a dark, quiet winter's night?

He gives his harness bells a shake
To ask if there is some mistake.

That wakes the guy up. He's been in a sort of trance, watching the snow fall. Yes, he'd like to stay there, the man realizes, but he has lots to do. He needs to get a move on.

Dad notices my lips moving. I explain about memorizing the poem, and he asks me to read it to him. He learns the last verse with me.

The woods are lovely, dark and deep,
But I have promises to keep,

And miles to go before I sleep,
And miles to go before I sleep.

Dad and I stop for supper at a roadside burger stand that has a million signs advertising huckleberry milkshakes. We each get one of those, along with burgers and, of course, onion rings. We sit at a picnic table under a willow tree.

"Did you ever notice that onion rings are always different sizes?" Dad asks.

"Yeah."

"I just realized why."

A bulb goes off in my head. An onion bulb. "I get it. It's a ball, and if you cut a ball in slices, you're going to have smaller slices at the edges. The very middle is the biggest, like the world's equator. But wait. Each slice has smaller and smaller rings inside it."

"I like the big ones, the equators," Dad says, lifting a large one to his mouth. The onion snakes out nude from its deep-fried batter casing, and he slurps it up.

"I like the small ones," I say. "The north pole and south pole." I pop a little brown O into my mouth.

"Then we'll get along like Jack Sprat and his wife," Dad says. He recites the nursery rhyme:

Jack Sprat could eat no fat.
His wife could eat no lean.
And so between the two of them,
They licked the platter clean.

The sun is going down and the air grows cool. As we walk back toward the truck, my throat tickles. That stupid tree air freshener.

Dad circles the truck, tightening the straps that keep the tarp snug over the large paper rolls, while I knock on every one of the truck's eighteen wheels with a hammer and listen closely. Every wheel rings out when I hit it. *Thud-CHIME.* If it doesn't chime, that means the tire needs air. It may even have a slow leak and need replacing. Luckily, all eighteen wheels are just fine.

We drive another three hours, listening to music and talking about this and that. Dad has a strict no-movies rule for the truck. "There's too much to look at out the window," he says. "Plus your eyes are needed. You've got to watch for hazards. Remember when you noticed that truck's tarp flapping?"

I did. Dad had radioed ahead to let the driver know things were coming loose from the bed of his truck.

In the dark, of course, there isn't much to see. I ask Dad about the dull lights that stud the highway's centerline. "RPMs," he says. "Reflective pavement markers. They're also called cat's eyes." The light from our headlights bounces off them and brightens up the road, letting us know we're on the right side of the highway. They're usually white and yellow, but Dad points out a green one by the side of the road. "That lets emergency vehicles know there's a hydrant nearby."

I look out for green RPMs for about ten miles, shouting, "Hydrant!" whenever we pass one.

"You just don't want to see red ones," Dad says.

"Why not?"

"They tell you you're going the wrong way."

Dad's watch beeps. "That's it for the night," he says. "There's a stop just up here."

Truck drivers are only allowed to drive for a certain number of hours a day. They have to get enough rest to drive safely.

We pull into a truck stop and plug in the kettle for tea. I put on one of

Dad's T-shirts to sleep in, and he gets into his pajamas. Nights on the road feel like camping. We take our mugs and walk, dressed like that, along a country road that takes us to a gurgling stream, where we crouch on the bank, listening to the crickets and the frogs creaking and croaking. "Peaceful," Dad says. He stands. "But miles to go."

We brush our teeth and pee in the truck-stop bathrooms, then walk quietly between the other trucks in the parking lot, where drivers lie in their cabs, some snoring, some listening to the radio, a few on their phones talking to friends.

Back at Dad's truck, I lower my bunk and climb into the sleeping bag that Grandma made by folding a patchwork quilt in half and stitching it up on two sides. Dad gets into his big bed below. There's lots of room behind the seats we've been sitting in all day. The cab of an eighteen-wheeler is mostly bed. Picture a car's back seat and trunk. Instead of those, imagine a bed.

Right behind Dad's seat, where your legs would be if you were in a car's back seat, there's a little fridge and, on the wall, a little cupboard. Something else that's different from a car is the ceiling is really high. That makes room for my bunk.

Dad writes in his log, and I transfer the day's onion-ring notes from the backs of napkins into a proper notebook.

Onion rings from Huckleberry Harry's
Crunch: just enough.
Came with dip!
Batter: light and flaky.

Dad: "The onion is sweet. Sometimes with onion rings, you can't taste the onion."
Jolene: "There's as much batter as onion. The onion isn't lost."
Dad: 8/10
Jolene: 8/10

"You have to cut the onion in the proper direction to turn it into rings," I say to Dad. "Onions grow in rings, like trees do."

"That sounds right."

"Do we grow like that too?"

Dad laughs. "In rings?"

"Well, it's spring again, and here I am on the road with you again. Everything repeats. Things go around and around."

"Hmm," Dad says. "I don't know. I just drove straight along a highway all day. So I think more about getting from point A to B rather than going around and around."

"But if you kept driving, you'd go around the world."

"And the wheels on the truck go around and around," Dad said.

"And the world goes around the sun. And every time it does, we get a year older. But we're the same person. Then one day we die."

Dad pretends he's shocked. "What?"

I laugh. "That guy in the poem saw it, I think. The end. Point B. But he's got to travel around and around a whole bunch more before he can just be still and watch the snow fall forever."

"The snowy woods," Dad says. "His version of heaven. I believe you're right, Genius Jolene."

Dad turns out the light and says good night. I lie in the sudden darkness, blinking long and slow, trying to decide if it's darker with my eyelids open or closed.

Chapter Five

When Dad's radio alarm goes off in the morning, the world feels heavy and dark, like a winter afternoon. A wind kicked up in the night.

Dad and I eat bagels with cream cheese from the little fridge and drink straight from the juice bottle so we don't have to wash any cups. Our plan is to drive for a few hours, then stop to eat in the middle of the morning.

"Breakunch," Dad says with a grin. "Or lunchfast?"

"Brunch!"

We start the day on a winding highway with forest and cliff on one side and the ocean on the other. We're singing along to one of Dad's favorite Red Hot Chili Peppers songs when all of a sudden, as we're rounding a corner, Dad gears down quickly.

"Holy God," he says, flinging an arm across me like a second seat belt. "Hold on!"

The truck shudders and screeches to a stop. Right in front of us, huge rocks are tumbling from the cliff above onto the highway. There's a horrible noise and clouds of brown dust. I plug my ears. I can *feel* when the rocks hit the road. Then, after just a moment, everything is quiet and still.

I feel like crying.

"Rockfall," Dad says. He cranes his neck and looks up at the cliff. "We're safe now." He unclasps his seat belt. "I'm going to hurry in there and make sure no one got hurt." He hands me his cell phone. "Dial 9-1-1."

I nod.

"Tell them what happened. Tell them everything you know, and don't worry about what you don't know. Okay?"

I nod. My heart is thudding.

"Sweetie, no one wants it to rain rocks, but we're fine," Dad says. "And there aren't a lot of people on the road today, so chances are good that no one got hurt. Can you reach under your seat and get the first-aid kit?"

I bend low and hand the kit to Dad.

He runs the windshield wipers to clear off the fresh layer of dust on the window, then opens his door. I find my voice as he steps down from the truck. "How do you know another big rock isn't going to come down? On you?"

"I trained for this when I was in the army. I'll be all right."

Dad reaches under his own seat and pulls out a yellow hard hat. "I'll be right back," he says in a helium voice, high and pinched. It's his joke every time he puts on a hat, as if it's squeezing him super tightly. I laugh, even in the middle of all the scary stuff.

As Dad heads into the dust, his hard hat glowing like a little sun, I press 9 and then 1 and then 1 again on the keypad. My finger is trembling. My whole body is shaking.

As the phone rings, I notice in the side mirror that a line of cars is gathering behind the truck.

"Emergency or nonemergency?" asks a voice on the other end of the line.

"Emergency, I think. Parts of a cliff fell onto the highway."

"That's an emergency, all right. What's your name?"

"Jolene."

"Nice name! How old are you?"

"Eight."

"Are there adults with you?"

"No. My dad's gone to see if anyone's hurt."

"Do you know what highway you're on, Jolene?"

I remember Dad telling Joey, and we've passed tons of signs. "Nineteen."

"Which direction?"

"Toward L.A. from—well, we woke up in Oregon."

"Can you put me on speaker and open Google Maps? Make sure data is turned on."

I do as she asks. "Yup."

"Now hold your finger on the screen until a window pops up."

"Got it."

"Okay. Read me the long number you see, with the dash in the middle of it."

I read the long number.

"Well done. Those are your global positioning coordinates. They let us know exactly where you are. What are you doing on Highway 19 anyway?"

"My dad's a trucker."

"My dad was a trucker too! Now, is your dad injured?"

"He's fine. He has taken the first-aid kit. He was a soldier and knows what to do."

"Okay. We're getting calls from other people who are there. Are rocks still tumbling?"

"No. There's just dust. Why did the rocks fall?"

"Gravity, I guess."

"Can I unroll my window?"

"Go ahead. A girl's got to breathe."

Dad comes out of the dust cloud with his arm around a woman. She has blood on her forehead and cheek. A boy about my age follows after them.

"It looks like my dad found some people who need help," I say into the phone. "A mom and a boy."

"Do they look all right?"

"They're both walking. But the woman's face is bleeding."

"Ask your dad if anyone else is hurt."

I yell out the window to Dad. He shakes his head.

"No."

"That's a good help. We've got ambulances on their way, on both sides of the fall. Can you leave your phone on? I'll call if I need more information."

"Yep."

"Enjoy the rest of your trip, Jolene," the woman says. "Remember, this is just a hiccup."

Dad calls me out of the truck and tells me to grab a blanket. I spread my patchwork quilt on the ground, and we sit the woman down. Dad examines her wounds.

Her face is pinched, like she's being brave but also like she's mad. The boy just stares quietly. He's wearing a striped shirt, the kind that buttons up, jeans and brown lace-up shoes like you might wear to a wedding or to church. Shoes you can't run in. The boy's looking at his mother like he's going to be sick.

"She's going to be fine," Dad tells him. "Are you hurt?"

The boy shakes his head.

"Your car is totaled," Dad says. "There's no changing that. But that's nothing compared to what could have happened to you. There's no one else in your car, right? No animals?"

The boy shakes his head again.

"Here." Dad hands the boy a bottle of water from the first-aid kit. "Drink. And get your mother to have some too."

Dad hands me a bottle of ointment and a cloth. "I want you to very gently clean away the blood. Just pat at her cuts. Don't rub. Their windshield broke, and we want to see if any glass is lodged in there. I'm going to get their bags."

The phone comes to life beside me as he's walking away. I put it on speaker. "This is the county," says a voice. "We got your number from 9-1-1."

"How can I help?" Dad asks.

"We understand you have some training. We're trying to figure out what we'll need in terms of road crews."

"It's only about eight boulders and a fair bit of debris, small rocks and gravel, easy to clear," Dad says. "The road looks damaged, but just in one lane. One car was hit, but the occupants aren't badly hurt. They may be in some shock. You'll have to tow their car."

I look at the boy. He just stares back.

"Ouch," the woman says as soon as I touch her with the cloth.

"Sorry," I say.

When they're cleaning a cut or pulling out a sliver, Mom and Dad always chat to distract me.

"I'm Jolene. What's your name?" I ask the woman.

"Claire Thomas. Mrs. Thomas. This is my son, Jeremy."

"Where were you heading?"

"My sister-in-law's." Mrs. Thomas flicks her thumb toward Jeremy. "He wanted to play Xbox with his cousins." She turns and looks at him. "Just had to play today, didn't you?"

Jeremy shrinks.

Mrs. Thomas looks up at the truck. "Riding along with your dad?"

"We're taking this load of newsprint down to L.A."

"Long drive."

"We do a trip together once a year. Mom never liked to travel with him, and neither does his boyfriend."

Mrs. Thomas jerks her head away from my cloth. "Boyfriend? Your dad has a *boyfriend*? That's disgusting. A sin."

My face stings like it's been slapped.

Mrs. Thomas stands. "Come on, Jeremy."

She crosses the highway to where a police car and ambulance are just arriving, driving along the shoulder past the line of stopped cars. As he follows after his mother, Jeremy stares back at me. When he finally stops looking, I grab the digital camera and take a photo of his and his mother's backs.

Chapter Six

The big rocks landed on only one lane of the highway. The road crews arrive, men and women in hard hats, heavy boots and orange vests. They quickly clear away the rubble from the other lane and open the road again.

The ambulance goes through first, with Mrs. Thomas and Jeremy inside. We're next. Road crews flag us along.

We drive past the fallen rocks and see the crumpled car with the smashed windshield. I take a picture.

"It's a miracle," Dad says, shaking his head. "They were very lucky."

"That's not a miracle," I say. "They lost their car, and she got cut up, and he doesn't get to go play Xbox with his cousins. It would have been a miracle if the rocks had missed them completely."

Dad looks at me in surprise. "Well, some see the cup half full and others see it half empty."

Ever since the woman stomped away, her words have repeated in my head. *Disgusting. Sin.* I burn every time I remember them.

"You okay?" Dad asks as we drive past the last flag person and back onto the wide highway again.

I shrug.

"It's a shock. In all my years of driving, I've never actually seen a rockfall happening. Hey, you know what?" He puts the turn signal on. "The hospital's just up there." We pass a blue sign with a large white H on it. "We should bring that woman some flowers. You're right, Jolene. They could have died. And she may need stitches on her face. You said some of the cuts looked deep."

My tongue won't move.

"It will just take a few minutes. We'll have to park on the side of the road. There won't be enough space for the rig in the parking lot."

I want to tell Dad what the woman said, but I can't say the words out loud, especially to him. He parks the truck with the hazard lights flashing and

hops out. "Come on, daughter. I can't leave the truck here for long."

Inside the hospital, a bony man at the information desk tells us Mrs. Thomas is in Emergency. He also points out a little store that sells balloons—*Get Well Soon! Congratulations!*—and gum and slippers and magazines, as well as flowers. Dad chooses a bouquet of pink and yellow flowers and heads to the cash register to pay. He gives me a funny smile. "You wait outside." I can tell he's hiding something from me.

I wait in the hallway, watching people come and go. It's weird. Everybody looks like they could suddenly snap at me. Dad comes out with the flowers and his jacket bundled up under his arm. Normally I'd dance around him, begging to see what was wrapped up inside it, but I can't get excited.

"What's up, Jo-Jo?" Dad asks. "You seem so worried. We're safe now. Think of the fencing you see on cliffs. That's to keep rocks from falling onto the road. Engineers are always looking out for potential rockfalls. This was just a freak thing. It won't happen again."

My eyes sting.

"Hey, it's okay," Dad says.

"It's not the rocks," I mumble.

"What is it, then?"

Tears fill my eyes, making everything blurry. "Let's go in there," Dad says. He leads me through a glass door to an outdoor garden where it's quiet and smells like dirt, but in a good way. We sit on a bench.

"I messed up," I finally say.

"You caused that rockfall?" Dad jokes.

"It's not funny."

"You're right. Sorry."

I take a breath and tell Dad everything. I tell him what I said, what Mrs. Thomas said, then how she got up and walked away. "Her face was even worse than her words. It was ugly, like she'd breathed in a really bad smell. Like *I* was a bad smell."

Dad is quiet for a moment. Then he turns and looks me square in the eyes. "Sweetheart, you did not mess up. The world messed up. Something's wrong if you can't talk about the people you love."

"I didn't want to tell you," I say. My chin wobbles. I don't want to bawl though. I want to be brave. I put my hand on my chin and hold it in place.

"You wanted to protect me. That was really kind of you."

"Are you mad?"

"At you? No!"

"At her?"

"Well, I'm mad she spread her hatred to you. That was not cool."

I look at the bouquet he bought. "What are we going to do with those?"

"Toss them?"

"Yeah!"

Dad laughs. "No, Jolene. We won't do that. We got the flowers for Mrs. Thomas."

I'm confused. "Why would we give something nice to someone who's mean?" I think about that space between the signs on the highway saying we're entering Martinville and leaving Martinville. My mind flashes two signs, one saying *Be nice*, the other, *Be mad*. "They tell us at school to walk away from bullies."

"That's wise. But we're not making friends with this woman. We're not saying we agree with her. We're just showing her some human kindness. She's been in a terrible accident. She's had an awful shock. Anyway, if we start acting the way she's acting, where does it end? They say it's better to light a candle than curse the darkness."

"What does that mean?"

"Well, if things are awful, you can complain about it all you want, but nothing will change. You've got to do something nice."

I look into the hospital. A person in scrubs is pushing a stretcher with someone on it. "Do doctors and nurses have to help everybody?"

"Yes. Even people who are rude and mean."

"But why are people rude and mean?"

"There are lots of reasons. They've been raised to believe mean things. They're frightened. They have been hurt and haven't healed, so they're angry. They've never been loved themselves."

"That happens?"

"I'm afraid so. Some people didn't win the lottery and get fantastic parents like you did."

"Ha ha," I say. "So people who weren't loved don't learn to love? It just keeps going?"

"No, actually. Sometimes that makes people *more* loving. They know how valuable love is." Dad takes my hand and stands. "Come on. Let's do this."

When we get to Emergency, we're led into a little room where Mrs. Thomas is lying on a bed, under a sheet. Jeremy sits close to the door, playing with a cell phone.

Mrs. Thomas sits up when we enter the room, but when she recognizes us, her face closes up like a wrinkled dishcloth.

"We wanted to give you our best wishes," Dad tells her.

"Take the flowers, Jeremy," Mrs. Thomas says.

Jeremy takes the flowers from us.

The woman says nothing more.

"Well, that's it then," Dad says. "Speedy recovery."

Mrs. Thomas looks at Dad as if it was his fault the rocks came down on her car, then looks away.

As we head out of the room, Jeremy pokes a finger into my waist. I look at him, shocked.

He tips his chin toward his mother's back, then looks back at me. *Sorry*, he mouths. He glances at Dad and nods, then smiles a small but true smile, and it's like when the sun rises over the horizon.

Chapter Seven

In the truck, Dad plops his bundled-up jacket onto my lap. I unroll it, and a crinkly bag falls out.

"Chips?" I say.

"Not just any chips!"

I read the writing on the bag. "*Golden Hoops?*"

I think of angels' halos and glowing basketball nets. I tear open the bag.

Inside are treats like chips, but the same shape and size as onion rings.

"Are these what the Raptors eat?" I ask. "Are these why they won the NBA championship?"

Dad laughs and plunges his hand into the bag.

Golden Hoops are salty and greasy and crunchy. There is no slippery onion, but the taste is definitely oniony. We polish them off long before the hospital is out of view.

"We're going to have to push to get to L.A. in time," Dad says. "We'll be driving late, burning the candle at both ends."

As usual when someone says that, I picture a candle with wicks lit on both the top and bottom. But as we drive, mile after mile, I get a chance to really think about it. And I figure it out!

"Before electricity, if you got up really early to do chores," I tell Dad, "you'd light a candle so you could see what you were doing. And if you worked late, you also had to light a candle. So you lit a candle at both ends *of the day*."

"That's got to be it. Genius Jolene!"

We only stop once all the way to L.A., at an enormous truck stop that has

not only a coin laundry and showers, but also a barbershop and a dentist!

The restaurant's menu lists onion *ringlets*, and Dad and I pounce on them. They're onion rings cut very thin, and they're freshly made. Because they're so thin, they don't hold the round shape but come out as wobbly ovals. I even get one that's a figure eight. They're totally delicious. The batter is not too crispy and not too dark or greasy. It flakes off a bit, which is annoying because you want to get every last bit and not be eating bare onion. They come with two sauces—aioli, which is mayonnaise with lots of garlic and is so delicious that Dad and I order two extra portions, and mayonnaise chipotle, which is quite spicy and which Dad thinks doesn't match the onion rings. I'm still deciding.

The ringlets rate 8.5 from each of us, our highest mark yet.

It's nearly midnight when we reach L.A. We don't drive into the city, but to a warehouse on the outskirts where we'll sleep and then unload the rolls of paper in the morning.

It's a warm night. We get our flashlights and follow a path up a hill. At the top is a view of shimmering L.A., its highways like red and white rivers from the cars' headlights and taillights. Dad points out the giant letters on a hillside that spell *HOLLYWOOD* and the row of palm trees, dark shapes against the sunset, that stretches along Hollywood Boulevard. I take two pictures.

"I can't believe we're already heading home tomorrow," I say.

"It always goes so fast when you're with me," Dad answers. "Spending time with you, my daughter, is a great joy in my life."

We stand there for a long time, listening to the distant sounds of the city and the sounds close by of birds settling in for the night. Finally we head back down the hill and tuck ourselves in too.

When I wake up, the paper rolls are already unloaded, and Dad's ready to head to a nearby warehouse to get the new load for our drive home. I climb directly from my bed into my seat.

After a few minutes we park, and Dad disappears into the warehouse. He comes out laughing. "You won't believe what we're carrying! Short sections of sewage pipe."

"Sewage isn't funny," I say.

"Wait until you see these things, and you'll know why I'm laughing."

While the warehouse workers get the new load onto the truck, I wander into the field behind the warehouse. Something is rustling in the long grass. I'm expecting a stray cat to show its tail, but instead two huge rats amble out. They have shaggy fur and white faces and little snouts. They're adorable.

They're opossums! Joey and I read a book about them. They have pouches, just like kangaroos do, to keep their newborns warm. And they're nocturnal, so it's getting past bedtime for these two.

I stay as still as I can, trying not to breathe, but they know I'm here. Opossums are excellent smellers since they hunt at night. The two little beasts turn their heads and sniff my way, and then hurry back into the long grass. A moment later, they're ambling up the trunk of a tree. It's not just any tree. It's like a Christmas tree, but it's *blue*. *A blue tree!* Once the opossums are lost high in the branches, I approach and put my nose to the tree's needles. The smell is really good and doesn't make my throat itch or my nose twitch. I break off a small branch.

The new load *is* hilarious. We're driving home five sections of concrete sewage pipe laid on their sides like enormous onion rings. Come to think of it, the rolls of paper were also like onion rings.

As Dad signs all the papers related to the new cargo, I take down the stinky, poisonous cardboard tree, wrap it in a plastic bag and stuff it into the glove compartment. In its place I hang the small branch from the blue tree.

"Is that blue spruce?" Dad asks as he buckles up his seatbelt.

I shrug. "That fake cardboard tree was bugging my nose and throat."

"Well, I guess natural is always better. That spruce is nice and fresh. Where did you find it?"

"Just behind the warehouse."

"See these?" Dad points to the ends of the twigs, which are lighter blue than the rest of the needles, and soft. "These are the buds, fresh this spring. Spruce tips are edible. Joey put them in a salad once and said they were packed with vitamin C. Have a nibble."

I pinch off a few of the soft needles and chew on them. They're kind of bitter,

but they're yummy too. They taste a lot like they smell.

"Not bad," I say.

"Joey wants to make spruce-tip ice cream one day, if you can believe it. I bet you blue-spruce tips would work too. Why don't you go grab a good handful and we'll bring him a little souvenir from L.A.?"

I'm a little nervous returning to the tree. I don't want to startle the opossums. They're not dangerous to people, but they will bare their teeth and hiss if they feel trapped. I look through the branches to see if they're still at the top of the tree.

As I crane my neck, I remember looking up when we drove through the debris from the rock fall. Dad had told me we were perfectly safe, but I needed to make sure. The top edge of the cliff looked clean and bright, like new. Then I remember the mean woman. But instead of her angry face, I see the flowers we got for her. They're bright, like a lantern. I'm glad we gave them to her. If we hadn't, I think I'd still feel afraid.

Four little eyes peer down from the top of the tree. Friendly, sleepy. "I'm just getting a few spruce tips," I sing up.

As I run back to the truck, I get a great idea. "When we get home, let's have Mom over and make onion rings and blue-spruce-tip ice cream for her and Joey," I tell Dad as I scramble back into my seat.

"Genius Jolene," Dad clucks. He puts the truck into gear. "Onward?"

"Onward," I agree.

"Miles to go—" Dad starts.

"—before we sleep."

Oven-Baked
Onion Rings

Usually, the onion rings you get in restaurants are fried in hot oil. That's definitely a big part of why they're so delicious. But oven-baked is easier to make and safer (no spattering oil).

You may need some help cutting the onions and getting the tray in and out of the oven, but that's it.

You'll need two baking sheets, two bowls, a whisk, a spoon, a spatula and a bunch of hunger. Preheat the oven to 375 degrees.

INGREDIENTS:

3	large white or yellow onions (or try purple as an experiment!)
2¼ cups	bread crumbs (ask at the bakery section of your supermarket)
¾ tsp	salt
1 tsp	garlic powder, or 1–2 garlic cloves, minced
3	eggs, beaten
Optional:	paprika

Slice the onion thickly IN THE CORRECT DIRECTION!! If you imagine the tip of the onion as a hat, slice it off, and keep slicing. Pop the little rings out of the big ones.

DIRECTIONS:

In a bowl, beat the eggs with a whisk until they're foamy. Crack the eggs open first!

Mix the bread crumbs, salt and garlic (and paprika) together in a separate bowl.

Take a ring and dip it in the egg.

Plop the wet ring into the breadcrumb mix on both sides so the crumbs and garlic stick to it. This is called *dredging*.

Put the wet, coated ring on a baking sheet.

Continue until the baking sheets are full (one layer of rings—don't stack!).

Place in oven, and bake for 20 minutes. If you get bored waiting, flip the rings halfway through the cooking time. This will help make sure they're evenly browned.

Serve with ketchup or mayonnaise or a mix of the two. Add a bit of hot sauce if you like that kind of thing. Ranch dressing is good too. Or make AIOLI SAUCE!

BONUS RECIPE: AIOLI SAUCE!

½ cup	mayonnaise
2 tsp	minced fresh garlic
2 tbsp	fresh lemon juice

Mix together. Ta-da! You can use bottled lemon juice and even powdered garlic, if that's all you've got.

EAT!

Spruce-Tip Syrup

You can chop up spruce tips and add them raw to salads or stir them into berries or ice cream. Remember they have a strong flavour. A little goes a long way!

In the spring, collect a few cups of young spruce buds, the soft new nubs at the ends of the tree's branches. They look like this:

All are safe to eat, but some are more bitter than others, so you may want to try a few to find the right tree. Forager Alan Bergo recommends packing water so you can rinse out your mouth if you need to! Bergo says to pick from older trees and never from the top of a tree.

Make this with a friend who is allowed to use the stove.

INGREDIENTS:

2 cups	spruce tips
2 cups	sugar
2 cups	water

DIRECTIONS:

Combine ingredients in a large pot and put on the stove over high heat.

When the water starts to bubble a little—to *simmer*—remove pot from stove, put the lid on, and let sit overnight. While you're sleeping, the flavour from the needles will travel into—*infuse*— the liquid.

The next day, pour your concoction through a colander to separate out the buds. Don't forget to put a bowl underneath to catch the precious liquid!

Return the liquid to the pot. Cook on medium-high heat, stirring until it is as thick as hot brown honey (but not too thick!).

Serve it hot or cold. It's good on vanilla, chocolate or berry ice cream, but try it on anything!

Store syrup in the refrigerator. If it gets too thick, thin it down with a bit of cold water.